THE DAY OF THE BOOMER DUKES

Start Publishing PD is a registered trademark of Start Publishing PD LLC
Manufactured in the United States of America

Cover art: Shutterstock/Taisiya Kozorez

Cover design: Jennifer Do

10 9 8 7 6 5 4 3 2 1

ISBN 979-8-8809-1463-0

THE DAY OF THE BOOMER DUKES

by Frederik Pohl

CONTENTS

FORAMINIFERA 9

Paptaste udderly, semped sempsemp dezhavoo, qued schmerz—Excuse me. I mean to say that it was like an endless diet of days, boring, tedious....

No, it loses too much in the translation. Explete my reasons, I say. Do my reasons matter? No, not to you, for you are troglodytes, knowing nothing of causes, understanding only acts. Acts and facts, I will give you acts and facts.

First you must know how I am called. My "name" is Foraminifera 9-Hart Bailey's Beam, and I am of adequate age and size. (If you doubt this, I am prepared to fight.) Once the—the tediety of life, as you might say, had made itself clear to me, there were, of course, only two alternatives. I do not like to die, so that possibility was out; and the remaining alternative was flight.

Naturally, the necessary machinery was available to me. I arrogated a small viewing machine, and scanned the centuries of the past in the hope that a sanctuary might reveal itself to my aching eyes. Kwel tediety that was! Back, back I went through the ages. Back to the Century of the Dog, back to the Age of the Crippled Men. I found no time better than my own. Back and back I peered, back as far as the Numbered Years. The Twenty-Eighth Century was boredom unendurable, the Twenty-Sixth a morass of dullness. Twenty-Fifth, Twenty-Fourth—wherever I looked, tediety was what I found.

*

I snapped off the machine and considered. Put the problem thus: Was there in all of the pages of history no age in which a 9-Hart Bailey's Beam might find adventure and excitement? There had to be! It was not possible, I told myself, despairing, that from the dawn of the dreaming primates until my own time there was no era at all in which I could be—happy? Yes, I suppose happiness is what I was looking for. But where was it? In my viewer, I had fifty centuries or more to look back upon. And that was, I decreed, the trouble; I could spend my life staring into the viewer, and yet never discover the time that was right for me. There were simply too many eras to choose from. It was like an enormous library in which there must, there had to be, contained the one fact I was looking for—that, lacking an index, I might wear my life away and never find.

"*Index!*"

I said the word aloud! For, to be sure, it was the answer. I had the freedom of the Learning Lodge, and the index in the reading room could easily find for me just what I wanted.

Splendid, splendid! I almost felt cheerful. I quickly returned the viewer I had been using to the keeper, and received my deposit back. I hurried to the Learning Lodge and fed my specifications into the index, as follows, that is to say: Find me a time in recent past where there is adventure and excitement, where there is a secret, colorful band of desperadoes with whom I can ally myself. I then added two specifications—second, that it should be before the time of the high radiation levels; and first, that it should be after the discovery of anesthesia, in case of accident—and retired to a desk in the reading room to await results.

It took only a few moments, which I occupied in making a list of the gear I wished to take with me. Then there was a hiss and a crackle, and in the receiver of the desk a book appeared. I unzipped the case, took it out, and opened it to the pages marked on the attached reading tape.

I had found my wonderland of adventure!

*

Ah, hours and days of exciting preparation! What a round of packing and buying; what a filling out of forms and a stamping of visas; what an orgy of injections and inoculations and preventive therapy! Merely getting ready for the trip made my pulse race faster and my adrenalin balance rise to the very point of paranoia; it was like being given a true blue new chance to live.

At last I was ready. I stepped into the transmission capsule; set the dials; unlocked the door, stepped out; collapsed the capsule and stored it away in my carry-all; and looked about at my new home.

Pyew! Kwel smell of staleness, of sourness, above all of coldness! It was a close matter then if I would be able to keep from a violent eructative stenosis, as you say. I closed my eyes and remembered warm violets for a moment, and then it was all right.

The coldness was not merely a smell; it was a physical fact. There was a damp grayish substance underfoot which I recognized as snow; and in a hard-surfaced roadway there were a number of wheeled vehicles moving, which caused the liquefying snow to splash about me. I adjusted my coat controls for warmth and deflection, but that was the best I could do. The reek of stale decay remained. Then there were also the buildings, painfully almost vertical. I believe it would not have disturbed me if they had been truly vertical; but many of them were minutes of arc from a true perpendicular, all of them covered with a carbonaceous material which I instantly perceived was an inadvertent deposit from the air. It was a bad beginning!

However, I was not *bored*.

*

I made my way down the "street," as you say, toward where a group of young men were walking toward me, five abreast. As I came near, they looked at me with interest and kwel respect, conversing with each other in whispers.

I addressed them: "Sirs, please direct me to the nearest recruiting office, as you call it, for the dread Camorra."

They stopped and pressed about me, looking at me intently. They were handsomely, though crudely dressed in coats of a striking orange color, and long trousers of an extremely dark material.

I decreed that I might not have made them understand me—it is always probable, it is understood, that a quicknik course in dialects of the past may not give one instant command of spoken communication in the field. I spoke again: "I wish to encounter a representative of the Camorra, in other words the Black Hand, in other words the cruel and sinister Sicilian terrorists named the Mafia. Do you know where these can be found?"

One of them said, "Nay. What's that jive?"

I puzzled over what he had said for a moment, but in the end decreed that his message was sensefree. As I was about to speak, however, he said suddenly: "Let's rove, man." And all five of them walked quickly away a few "yards." It was quite disappointing. I observed them conferring among themselves, glancing at me, and for a time proposed terminating my venture, for I then believed that it would be better to return "home," as you say, in order to more adequately research the matter.

*

However, the five young men came toward me again. The one who had spoken before, who I now detected was somewhat taller and fatter than the others, spoke as follows: "You're wanting the Mafia?" I agreed. He looked at me for a moment. "Are you holding?"

He was inordinately hard to understand. I said, slowly and with patience, "Keska that 'holding' say?"

"Money, man. You going to slip us something to help you find these cats?"

"Certainly, money. I have a great quantity of money instantly available," I rejoined him. This appeared to relieve his mind.

There was a short pause, directly after which this first of the young men spoke: "You're on, man. Yeah, come with us. What's to call you?" I queried this last statement, and he expanded: "The name. What's the name?"

"You may call me Foraminifera 9," I directed, since I wished to be incognito, as you put it, and we proceeded along the "street." All five of the young men indicated a desire to serve me, offering indeed to take my carry-all. I rejected this, politely.

I looked about me with lively interest, as you may well believe. Kwel dirt, kwel dinginess, kwel cold! And yet there was a certain charm which I can determine no way of expressing in this language. Acts and facts, of course. I shall not attempt to capture the subjectivity which is the charm, only to transcribe the physical datum—perhaps even data, who knows? My companions, for example: They were in appearance overwrought, looking about them continually, stopping entirely and drawing me with them into the shelter of a "door" when another man, this one wearing blue clothing and a visored hat appeared. Yet they were clearly devoted to me, at that moment, since they had put aside their own projects in order to escort me without delay to the Mafia.

*

Mafia! Fortunate that I had found them to lead me to the Mafia! For it had been clear in the historical work I had consulted that it was not ultimately easy to gain access to the Mafia. Indeed, so secret were they that I had detected no trace of their existence in other histories of the period. Had I relied only on the conventional work, I might never have known of their great underground struggle against what you term society. It was only in the actual contemporary volume itself, the curiosity titled *U.S.A. Confidential* by one Lait and one Mortimer, that I had descried that, throughout the world, this great revolutionary organization flexed its tentacles, the plexus within a short distance of where I now stood, battling courageously. With me to help them, what heights might we not attain! Kwel dramatic delight!

My meditations were interrupted. "Boomers!" asserted one of my five escorts in a loud, frightened tone. "Let's cut, man!" he continued, leading me with them into another entrance. It appeared, as well as I could decree, that the cause of his ejaculative outcry was the discovery of perhaps three, perhaps four, other young men, in coats of the same shiny material as my escorts. The difference was that they were of a different color, being blue.

*

We hastened along a lengthy chamber which was quite dark, immediately after which the large, heavy one opened a way to a serrated incline leading downward. It was extremely dark, I should say. There was also an extreme smell, quite like that of the outer air, but enormously intensified; one would suspect that there was an incomplete combustion of, perhaps, wood or coal, as well as a certain quantity of general decay. At any rate, we reached the bottom of the incline, and my escort behaved quite badly. One of them said to the other four, in these words: "Them jumpers follow us sure. Yeah, there's much trouble. What's to prime this guy now and split?"

Instantly they fell upon me with violence. I had fortunately become rather alarmed at their visible emotion of fear, and already had taken from my carry-all a Stollgratz 16, so that I quickly turned it on them. I started to replace the Stollgratz 16 as they fell to the floor, yet I realized that there might be an additional element of danger. Instead of putting the Stollgratz 16 in with the other trade goods, which I had brought to assist me in negotiating with the Mafia, I transferred it to my jacket. It had become clear to me that the five young men of my escort had intended to abduct and rob me—indeed had intended it all along, perhaps having never intended to convoy me to the office of the Mafia. And the other young men, those who wore the blue jackets in place of the orange, were already descending the incline toward me, quite rapidly.

"Stop," I directed them. "I shall not entrust myself to you until you have given me evidence that you entirely deserve such trust."

*

They all halted, regarding me and the Stollgratz 16. I detected that one of them said to another: "That cat's got a zip."

The other denied this, saying: "That no zip, man. Yeah, look at them Leopards. Say, you bust them flunkies with that thing?"

I perceived his meaning quite quickly. "You are 'correct'," I rejoined. "Are you associated in friendship with them flunkies?"

"Hell, no. Yeah, they're Leopards and we're Boomer Dukes. You cool them, you do us much good." I received this information as indicating that the two socio-economic units were inimical, and unfortunately lapsed into an example of the Bivalent Error. Since p implied not-q, I sloppily assumed that not-q implied r (with, you understand, r being taken as the class of phenomena pertinently favorable to me). This was a very poor construction, and of course resulted in certain difficulties. Qued, after all. I stated:

"Them flunkies offered to conduct me to a recruiting office, as you say, of the Mafia, but instead tried to take from me the much money I am holding." I then went on to describe to them my desire to attain contact with the said Mafia; meanwhile they descended further and grouped about me in the very little light, examining curiously the motionless figures of the Leopards.

They seemed to be greatly impressed; and at the same time, very much puzzled. Naturally. They looked at the Leopards, and then at me.

They gave every evidence of wishing to help me; but of course if I had not forgotten that one cannot assume from the statements "not-Leopard implies Boomer Duke" and "not-Leopard implies Foraminifera 9" that, qued, "Boomer Duke implies Foraminifera 9" ... if I had not forgotten this, I say, I should not have been "deceived." For in practice they were as little favorable to me as the Leopards. A certain member of their party reached a position behind me.

I quickly perceived that his intention was not favorable, and attempted to turn around in order to discharge at him with the Stollgratz 16, but he was very rapid. He had a metallic cylinder, and with it struck my head, knocking "me" unconscious.

SHIELD 8805

This candy store is called Chris's. There must be ten thousand like it in the city. A marble counter with perhaps five stools, a display case of cigars and a bigger one of candy, a few dozen girlie magazines hanging by clothespin-sort-of things from wire ropes along the wall. It has a couple of very small glass-topped tables under the magazines. And a juke—I can't imagine a place like Chris's without a juke.

I had been sitting around Chris's for a couple of hours, and I was beginning to get edgy. The reason I was sitting around Chris's was not that I liked Cokes particularly, but that it was one of the hanging-out places of a juvenile gang called The Leopards, with whom I had been trying to work for nearly a year; and the reason I was becoming edgy was that I didn't see any of them there.

The boy behind the counter—he had the same first name as I, Walter in both cases, though my last name is Hutner and his is, I believe, something Puerto Rican—the boy behind the counter was dummying up, too. I tried to talk to him, on and off, when he wasn't busy. He wasn't busy most of the time; it was too cold for sodas. But he just didn't want to talk. Now, these kids love to talk. A lot of what they say doesn't make sense—either bullying, or bragging, or purposeless swearing—but talk is their normal state; when they quiet down it means trouble. For instance, if you ever find yourself walking down Thirty-Fifth Street and a couple of kids pass you, talking, you don't have to bother looking around; but if they stop talking, turn quickly. You're about to be mugged. Not that Walt was a mugger—as far as I know; but that's the pattern of the enclave.

*

So his being quiet was a bad sign. It might mean that a rumble was brewing—and that meant that my work so far had been pretty nearly a failure. Even worse, it might mean that somehow the Leopards had discovered that I had at last passed my examinations and been appointed to the New York City Police Force as a rookie patrolman, Shield 8805.

Trying to work with these kids is hard enough at best. They don't like outsiders. But they particularly hate cops, and I had been trying for some weeks to decide how I could break the news to them.

The door opened. Hawk stood there. He didn't look at me, which was a bad sign. Hawk was one of the youngest in the Leopards, a skinny, very dark kid who had been reasonably friendly to me. He stood in the open door, with snow blowing in past him. "Walt. Out here, man."

It wasn't me he meant—they call me "Champ," I suppose because I beat them all shooting eight-ball pool. Walt put down the comic he had been reading and walked out, also without looking at me. They closed the door.

*

Time passed. I saw them through the window, talking to each other, looking at me. It was something, all right. They were scared. That's bad, because these kids are like wild animals; if you scare them, they hit first—it's the only way they know to defend themselves. But on the other hand, a rumble wouldn't scare them—not where they would show it; and finding out about the shield in my pocket wouldn't scare them, either. They hated cops, as I say; but cops were a part of their environment. It was strange, and baffling.

Walt came back in, and Hawk walked rapidly away. Walt went behind the counter, lit a cigaret, wiped at the marble top, picked up his comic, put it down again and finally looked at me. He said: "Some punk busted Fayo and a couple of the boys. It's real trouble."

I didn't say anything.

He took a puff on his cigaret. "They're chilled, Champ. Five of them."

"Chilled? Dead?" It sounded bad; there hadn't been a real rumble in months, not with a killing.

He shook his head. "Not dead. You're wanting to see, you go down Gomez's cellar. Yeah, they're all stiff but they're breathing. I be along soon as the old man comes back in the store."

He looked pretty sick. I left it at that and hurried down the block to the tenement where the Gomez family lived, and then I found out why.

*

They were sprawled on the filthy floor of the cellar like winoes in an alley. Fayo, who ran the gang; Jap; Baker; two others I didn't know as well. They were breathing, as Walt had said, but you just couldn't wake them up.

Hawk and his twin brother, Yogi, were there with them, looking scared. I couldn't blame them. The kids looked perfectly all right, but it was obvious that they weren't. I bent down and smelled, but there was no trace of liquor or anything else on their breath.

I stood up. "We'd better get a doctor."

"Nay. You call the meat wagon, and a cop comes right with it, man," Yogi said, and his brother nodded.

I laid off that for a moment. "What happened?"

Hawk said, "You know that witch Gloria, goes with one of the Boomer Dukes? She opened her big mouth to my girl. Yeah, opened her mouth and much bad talk came out. Said Fayo primed some jumper with a zip and the punk cooled him, and then a couple of the Boomers moved in real cool. Now they got the punk with the zip and much other stuff, real stuff."

"What kind of stuff?"

Hawk looked worried. He finally admitted that he didn't know what kind of stuff, but it was something dangerous in the way of weapons. It had been the "zip" that had knocked out the five Leopards.

I sent Hawk out to the drug-store for smelling salts and containers of hot black coffee—not that I knew what I was doing, of course, but they were dead set against calling an ambulance. And the boys didn't seem to be in any particular danger, only sleep.

*

However, even then I knew that this kind of trouble was something I couldn't handle alone. It was a tossup what to do—the smart thing was to call the precinct right then and there; but I couldn't help feeling that that would make the Leopards clam up hopelessly. The six months I had spent trying to work with them had not been too successful—a lot of the other neighborhood workers had made a lot more progress than I—but at least they were willing to talk to me; and they wouldn't talk to uniformed police.

Besides, as soon as I had been sworn in, the day before, I had begun the practice of carrying my .38 at all times, as the regulations say. It was in my coat. There was no reason for me to feel I needed it. But I did. If there was any truth to the story of a "zip" knocking out the boys—and I had all five of them right there for evidence—I had the unpleasant conviction that there was real trouble circulating around East Harlem that afternoon.

"Champ. They all waking up!"

I turned around, and Hawk was right. The five Leopards, all of a sudden, were stirring and opening their eyes. Maybe the smelling salts had something to do with it, but I rather think not.

We fed them some of the black coffee, still reasonably hot. They were scared; they were more scared than anything I had ever seen in those kids before. They could hardly talk at first, and when finally they came around enough to tell me what had happened I could hardly believe them. This man had been small and peculiar, and he had been looking for, of all things, the "Mafia," which he had read about in history books—*old* history books.

Well, it didn't make sense, unless you were prepared to make a certain assumption that I refused to make. Man from Mars? Nonsense. Or from the future? Equally ridiculous....

*

Then the five Leopards, reviving, began to walk around. The cellar was dark and dirty, and packed with the accumulation of generations in the way of old furniture and rat-inhabited mattresses and piles of newspapers; it wasn't surprising that we hadn't noticed the little gleaming thing that had apparently rolled under an abandoned potbelly stove.

Jap picked it up, squalled, dropped it and yelled for me.

I touched it cautiously, and it tingled. It wasn't painful, but it was an odd, unexpected feeling—perhaps you've come across the "buzzers" that novelty stores sell which, concealed in the palm, give a sudden, surprising tingle when the owner shakes hands with an unsuspecting friend. It was like that, like a mild electric shock. I picked it up and held it. It gleamed brightly, with a light of its own; it was round; it made a faint droning sound; I turned it over, and it spoke to me. It said in a friendly, feminine whisper: *Warning, this portatron attuned only to Bailey's Beam percepts. Remain quiescent until the Adjuster comes.*

That settled it. Any time a lit-up cue ball talks to me, I refer the matter to higher authority. I decided on the spot that I was heading for the precinct house, no matter what the Leopards thought.

But when I turned and headed for the stairs, I couldn't move. My feet simply would not lift off the ground. I twisted, and stumbled, and fell in a heap; I yelled for help, but it didn't do any good. The Leopards couldn't move either.

We were stuck there in Gomez's cellar, as though we had been nailed to the filthy floor.

COW

When I see what this flunky has done to them Leopards, I call him a cool cat right away. But then we jump him and he ain't so cool. Angel and Tiny grab him under the arms and I'm grabbing the stuff he's carrying. Yeah, we get out of there.

There's bulls on the street, so we cut through the back and over the fences. Tiny don't like that. He tells me, "Cow. What's to leave this cat here? He must weigh eighteen tons." "You're bringing him," I tell him, so he shuts up. That's how it is in the Boomer Dukes. When Cow talks, them other flunkies shut up fast.

We get him in the loft over the R. and I. Social Club. Damn, but it's cold up there. I can hear the pool balls clicking down below so I pass the word to keep quiet. Then I give this guy the foot and pretty soon he wakes up.

As soon as I talk to him a little bit I figure we had luck riding with us when we see them Leopards. This cat's got real bad stuff. Yeah, I never hear of anything like it. But what it takes to make a fight he's got. I take my old pistol and give it to Tiny. Hell, it makes him happy and what's it cost me? Because what this cat's got makes that pistol look like something for babies.

*

First he don't want to talk. "Stomp him," I tell Angel, but he's scared. He says, "Nay. This is a real weird cat, Cow. I'm for cutting out of here."

"Stomp him," I tell him again, pretty quiet, but he does it. He don't have to tell me this cat's weird, but when the cat gets the foot a couple of times he's willing to talk. Yeah, he talks real funny, but that don't matter to me. We take all the loot out of his bag, and I make this cat tell me what it's to do. Damn, I don't know what he's talking about one time out of six, but I know enough. Even Tiny catches on after a while, because I see him put down that funky old pistol I gave him that he's been loving up.

I'm feeling pretty good. I wish a couple of them chicken Leopards would turn up so I could show them what they missed out on. Yeah, I'll take on them, and the Black Dogs, and all the cops in the world all at once—that's how good I'm feeling. I feel so good that I don't even like it when Angel lets out a yell and comes up with a wad of loot. It's like I want to prime the U.S. Mint for chickenfeed, I don't want it to come so easy.

But money's on hand, so I take it off Angel and count it. This cat was really loaded; there must be a thousand dollars here.

I take a handful of it and hand it over to Angel real cool. "Get us some charge," I tell him. "There's much to do and I'm feeling ready for some charge to do it with."

"How many sticks you want me to get?" he asks, holding on to that money like he never saw any before.

I tell him: "Sticks? Nay. I'm for real stuff tonight. You find Four-Eye and get us some horse." Yeah, he digs me then. He looks like he's pretty scared and I know he is, because this punk hasn't had anything bigger than reefers in his life. But I'm for busting a couple of caps of H, and what I do he's going to do. He takes off to find Four-Eye and the rest of us get busy on this cat with the funny artillery until he gets back.

*

It's like I'm a million miles down Dream Street. Hell, I don't want to wake up.

But the H is wearing off and I'm feeling mean. Damn, I'll stomp my mother if she talks big to me right then.

I'm the first one on my feet and I'm looking for trouble. The whole place is full now. Angel must have passed the word to everybody in the Dukes, but I don't even remember them coming in. There's eight or ten cats lying around on the floor now, not even moving. This won't do, I decide.

If I'm on my feet, they're all going to be on their feet. I start to give them the foot and they begin to move. Even the weirdie must've had some H. I'm guessing that somebody slipped him some to see what would happen, because he's off on Cloud Number Nine. Yeah, they're feeling real mean when they wake up, but I handle them cool. Even that little flunky Sailor starts to go up against me but I look at him cool and he chickens. Angel and Pete are real sick, with the shakes and the heaves, but I ain't waiting for them to feel good. "Give me that loot," I tell Tiny, and he hands over the stuff we took off the weirdie. I start to pass out the stuff.

"What's to do with this stuff?" Tiny asks me, looking at what I'm giving him.

I tell him, "Point it and shoot it." He isn't listening when the weirdie's telling me what the stuff is. He wants to know what it does, but I don't know that. I just tell him, "Point it and shoot it, man." I've sent one of the cats out for drinks and smokes and he's back by then, and we're all beginning to feel a little better, only still pretty mean. They begin to dig me.

"Yeah, it sounds like a rumble," one of them says, after a while.

I give him the nod, cool. "You're calling it," I tell him. "There's much fighting tonight. The Boomer Dukes is taking on the world!"

SANDY VAN PELT

The front office thought the radio car would give us a break in spot news coverage, and I guessed as wrong as they did. I had been covering City Hall long enough, and that's no place to build a career—the Press Association is very tight there, there's not much chance of getting any kind of exclusive story because of the sharing agreements. So I put in for the radio car. It meant taking the night shift, but I got it.

I suppose the front office got their money's worth, because they played up every lousy auto smash the radio car covered as though it were the story of the Second Coming, and maybe it helped circulation. But I had been on it for four months and, wouldn't you know it, there wasn't a decent murder, or sewer explosion, or running gun fight between six P.M. and six A.M. any night I was on duty in those whole four months. What made it worse, the kid they gave me as photographer—Sol Detweiler, his name was—couldn't drive worth a damn, so I was stuck with chauffeuring us around.

We had just been out to LaGuardia to see if it was true that Marilyn Monroe was sneaking into town with Aly Khan on a night plane—it wasn't—and we were coming across the Triborough Bridge, heading south toward the East River Drive, when the office called. I pulled over and parked and answered the radiophone.

*

It was Harrison, the night City Editor. "Listen, Sandy, there's a gang fight in East Harlem. Where are you now?"

It didn't sound like much to me, I admit. "There's always a gang fight in East Harlem, Harrison. I'm cold and I'm on my way down to Night Court, where there may or may not be a story; but at least I can get my feet warm."

"*Where are you now?*" Harrison wasn't fooling. I looked at Sol, on the seat next to me; I thought I had heard him snicker. He began to fiddle with his camera without looking at me. I pushed the "talk" button and told Harrison where I was. It pleased him very much; I wasn't more than six blocks from where this big rumble was going on, he told me, and he made it very clear that I was to get on over there immediately.

I pulled away from the curb, wondering why I had ever wanted to be a newspaperman; I could have made five times as much money for half as much work in an ad agency. To make it worse, I heard Sol chuckle again. The reason he was so amused was that when we first teamed up I made the mistake of telling him what a hot reporter I was, and I had been visibly cooling off before his eyes for a better than four straight months.

Believe me, I was at the very bottom of my career that night. For five cents cash I would have parked the car, thrown the keys in the East River, and taken the first bus out of town. I was absolutely positive that the story would be a bust and all I would get out of it would be a bad cold from walking around in the snow.

And if that doesn't show you what a hot newspaperman I really am, nothing will.

*

Sol began to act interested as we reached the corner Harrison had told us to go to. "That's Chris's," he said, pointing at a little candy store. "And that must be the pool hall where the Leopards hang out."

"You know this place?"

He nodded. "I know a man named Walter Hutner. He and I went to school together, until he dropped out, couple weeks ago. He quit college to go to the Police Academy. He wanted to be a cop."

I looked at him. "You're going to college?"

"Sure, Mr. Van Pelt. Wally Hutner was a sociology major—I'm journalism—but we had a couple of classes together. He had a part-time job with a neighborhood council up here, acting as a sort of adult adviser for one of the gangs."

"They need advice on how to be gangs?"

"No, that's not it, Mr. Van Pelt. The councils try to get their workers accepted enough to bring the kids in to the social centers, that's all. They try to get them off the streets. Wally was working with a bunch called the Leopards."

I shut him up. "Tell me about it later!" I stopped the car and rolled down a window, listening.

*

Yes, there was something going on all right. Not at the corner Harrison had mentioned—there wasn't a soul in sight in any direction. But I could hear what sounded like gunfire and yelling, and, my God, even bombs going off! And it wasn't too far away. There were sirens, too—squad cars, no doubt.

"It's over that way!" Sol yelled, pointing. He looked as though he was having the time of his life, all keyed up and delighted. He didn't have to tell me where the noise was coming from, I could hear for myself. It sounded like D-Day at Normandy, and I didn't like the sound of it.

I made a quick decision and slammed on the brakes, then backed the car back the way we had come. Sol looked at me. "What—"

"Local color," I explained quickly. "This the place you were talking about? Chris's? Let's go in and see if we can find some of these hoodlums."

"But, Mr. Van Pelt, all the pictures are over where the fight's going on!"

"Pictures, shmictures! Come on!" I got out in front of the candy store, and the only thing he could do was follow me.

Whatever they were doing, they were making the devil's own racket about it. Now that I looked a little more closely I could see that they must have come this way; the candy store's windows were broken; every other street light was smashed; and what had at first looked like a flight of steps in front of a tenement across the street wasn't anything of the kind—it was a pile of bricks and stone from the false-front cornice on the roof! How in the world they had managed to knock that down I had no idea; but it sort of convinced me that, after all, Harrison had been right about this being a *big* fight.

Over where the noise was coming from there were queer flashing lights in the clouds overhead—reflecting exploding flares, I thought.

*

No, I didn't want to go over where the pictures were. I like living. If it had been a normal Harlem rumble with broken bottles and knives, or maybe even home-made zip guns—I might have taken a chance on it, but this was for real.

"Come on," I yelled to Sol, and we pushed the door open to the candy store.

At first there didn't seem to be anyone in, but after we called a couple times a kid of about sixteen, coffee-colored and scared-looking, stuck his head up above the counter.

"You. What's going on here?" I demanded. He looked at me as if I was some kind of a two-headed monster. "Come on, kid. Tell us what happened."

"Excuse me, Mr. Van Pelt." Sol cut in ahead of me and began talking to the kid in Spanish. It got a rise out of him; at least Sol got an answer. My Spanish is only a little bit better than my Swahili, so I missed what was going on, except for an occasional word. But Sol was getting it all. He reported: "He knows Walt; that's what's bothering him. He says Walt and some of the Leopards are in a basement down the street, and there's something wrong with them. I can't exactly figure out what, but—"

"The hell with them. What about *that*?"

"You mean the fight? Oh, it's a big one all right, Mr. Van Pelt. It's a gang called the Boomer Dukes. They've got hold of some real guns somewhere—I can't exactly understand what kind of guns he means, but it sounds like something serious. He says they shot that parapet down across the street. Gosh, Mr. Van Pelt, you'd think it'd take a cannon for something like that. But it has something to do with Walt Hutner and all the Leopards, too."

I said enthusiastically, "Very good, Sol. That's fine. Find out where the cellar is, and we'll go interview Hutner."

"But Mr. Van Pelt, the pictures—"

"Sorry. I have to call the office." I turned my back on him and headed for the car.

*

The noise was louder, and the flashes in the sky brighter—it looked as though they were moving this way. Well, I didn't have any money tied up in the car, so I wasn't worried about leaving it in the street. And somebody's cellar seemed like a very good place to be. I called the office and started to tell Harrison what we'd found out; but he stopped me short. "Sandy, where've you been? I've been trying to call you for—Listen, we got a call from Fordham. They've detected radiation coming from the East Side—it's got to be what's going on up there! Radiation, do you hear me? That means atomic weapons! Now, you get th—"

Silence.

"Hello?" I cried, and then remembered to push the talk button. "Hello? Harrison, you there?"

Silence. The two-way radio was dead.

I got out of the car; and maybe I understood what had happened to the radio and maybe I didn't. Anyway, there was something new shining in the sky. It hung below the clouds in parts, and I could see it through the bottom of the clouds in the middle; it was a silvery teacup upside down, a hemisphere over everything.

It hadn't been there two minutes before.

*

I heard firing coming closer and closer. Around a corner a bunch of cops came, running, turning, firing; running, turning and firing again. It was like the retreat from Caporetto in miniature. And what was chasing them? In a minute I saw. Coming around the corner was a kid with a lightning-blue satin jacket and two funny-looking guns in his hand; there was a silvery aura around him, the same color as the lights in the sky; and I swear I saw those cops' guns hit him twenty times in twenty seconds, but he didn't seem to notice.

Sol and the kid from the candy store were right beside me. We took another look at the one-man army that was coming down the street toward us, laughing and prancing and firing those odd-looking guns. And then the three of us got out of there, heading for the cellar. Any cellar.

PRIAM'S MAW

My occupation was "short-order cook", as it is called. I practiced it in a locus entitled "The White Heaven," established at Fifth Avenue, Newyork, between 1949 and 1962 C.E. I had created rapport with several of the aboriginals, who addressed me as Bessie, and presumed to approve the manner in which I heated specimens of minced ruminant quadruped flesh (deceased to be sure). It was a satisfactory guise, although tiring.

Using approved techniques, I was compiling anthropometric data while "I" was, as they say, "brewing coffee." I deem the probability nearly conclusive that it was the double duty, plus the datum that, as stated, "I" was physically tired, which caused me to overlook the first signal from my portatron. Indeed, I might have overlooked the second as well except that the aboriginal named Lester stated: "Hey, Bessie. Ya got an alarm clock in ya pocketbook?" He had related the annunciator signal of the portatron to the only significant datum in his own experience which it resembled, the ringing of a bell.

I annotated his dossier to provide for his removal in case it eventuated that he had made an undesirable intuit (this proved unnecessary) and retired to the back of the "store" with my carry-all. On identifying myself to the portatron, I received information that it was attuned to a Bailey's Beam, identified as Foraminifera 9-Hart, who had refused treatment for systemic weltschmerz and instead sought to relieve his boredom by adventuring into this era.

I thereupon compiled two recommendations which are attached: 2, a proposal for reprimand to the Keeper of the Learning Lodge for failure to properly annotate a volume entitled *U.S.A. Confidential* and, 1, a proposal for reprimand to the Transport Executive, for permitting Bailey's Beam-class personnel access to temporal transport. Meanwhile, I left the "store" by a rear exit and directed myself toward the locus of the transmitting portatron.

*

I had proximately left when I received an additional information, namely that developed weapons were being employed in the area toward which I was directing. This provoked that I abandon guise entirely. I went transparent and quickly examined all aboriginals within view, to determine if any required removal; but none had observed this. I rose to perhaps seventy-five meters and sped at full atmospheric driving speed toward the source of the alarm. As I crossed a "park" I detected the drive of another Adjuster, whom I determined to be Alephplex Priam's Maw—that is, my father. He bespoke me as follows: "Hurry, Besplex Priam's Maw. That crazy Foraminifera has been captured by aboriginals and they have taken his weapons away from him." "Weapons?" I inquired. "Yes, weapons," he stated, "for Foraminifera 9-Hart brought with him more than forty-three kilograms of weapons, ranging up to and including electronic."

I recorded this datum and we landed, went opaque in the shelter of a doorway and examined our percepts. "Quarantine?" asked my father, and I had to agree. "Quarantine," I voted, and he opened his carry-all and set-up a quarantine shield on the console. At once appeared the silvery quarantine dome, and the first step of our adjustment was completed. Now to isolate, remove, replace.

Queried Alephplex: "An Adjuster?" I observed the phenomenon to which he was referring. A young, dark aboriginal was coming toward us on the "street," driving a group of police aboriginals before him. He was armed, it appeared, with a fission-throwing weapon in one hand and some sort of tranquilizer—I deem it to have been a Stollgratz 16—in the other; moreover, he wore an invulnerability belt. The police aboriginals were attempting to strike him with missile weapons, which the belt deflected. I neutralized his shield, collapsed him and stored him in my carry-all. "Not an Adjuster," I asserted my father, but he had already perceived that this was so. I left him to neutralize and collapse the police aboriginals while I zeroed in on the portatron. I did not envy him his job with the police aboriginals, for many of them were "dead," as they say. It required the most delicate adjustments.

*

The portatron developed to be in a "cellar" and with it were some nine or eleven aboriginals which it had immobilized pending my arrival. One spoke to me thus: "Young lady, please call the cops! We're stuck here, and—" I did not wait to hear what he wished to say further, but neutralized and collapsed him with the other aboriginals. The portatron apologized for having caused me inconvenience; but of course it was not its fault, so I did not neutralize it. Using it for d-f, I quickly located the culprit, Foraminifera 9-Hart Bailey's Beam, nearby. He spoke despairingly in the dialect of the locus, "Besplex Priam's Maw, for God's sake get me out of this!" "Out!" I spoke to him, "you'll wish you never were 'born,' as they say!" I neutralized but did not collapse him, pending instructions from the Central Authority. The aboriginals who were with him, however, I did collapse.

Presently arrived Alephplex, along with four other Adjusters who had arrived before the quarantine shield made it not possible for anyone else to enter the disturbed area. Each one of us had had to abandon guise, so that this locus of Newyork 1939-1986 must require new Adjusters to replace us—a matter to be charged against the guilt of Foraminifera 9-Hart Bailey's Beam, I deem.

*

This concluded Steps 3 and 2 of our Adjustment, the removal and the isolation of the disturbed specimens. We are transmitting same disturbed specimens to you under separate cover herewith, in neutralized and collapsed state, for the manufacture of simulacra thereof. One regrets to say that they number three thousand eight hundred forty-six, comprising all aboriginals within the quarantined area who had first-hand knowledge of the anachronisms caused by Foraminifera's importation of contemporary weapons into this locus.

Alephplex and the four other Adjusters are at present reconstructing such physical damage as was caused by the use of said weapons. Simultaneously, while I am preparing this report, "I" am maintaining the quarantine shield which cuts off this locus, both physically and temporally, from the remainder of its environment. I deem that if replacements for the attached aboriginals can be fabricated quickly enough, there will be no significant outside percept of the shield itself, or of the happenings within it—that is, by maintaining a quasi-stasis of time while the repairs are being made, an outside aboriginal observer will see, at most, a mere flicker of silver in the sky. All Adjusters here present are working as rapidly as we can to make sure the shield can be withdrawn, before so many aboriginals have observed it as to make it necessary to replace the entire city with simulacra. We do not wish a repetition of the California incident, after all.

www.ingramcontent.com/pod-product-compliance
Lightning Source LLC
Chambersburg PA
CBHW050920120626
46552CB00004B/1681